"AMANDA, WHY SO QUIET?" her mother asked as they drove along the trail.

"Oh, I was just thinking," Mandie replied.

"Thinking about what?"

"Mrs. Chapman taking a job way off somewhere. Faith would have to move away," Mandie said.

"I know it's hard to lose a friend, but just think what this will do for Mrs. Chapman if she is able to secure the position," Mrs. Shaw said. "She will be able to earn a living for herself and Faith. And after losing all her family in that fire back in Missouri, she has no one but Faith. She needs Faith worse than we need her."

Mandie looked up at her mother. "I know, Mama. I'm glad for Mrs. Chapman, and Faith seems to be glad about it too, even though she knows she will have to move."

"Don't worry about losing a friend. You and Faith can always visit, and you will make more friends in the future," Mrs. Shaw promised.

"Maybe someone will move into their old house if they leave here," Mandie said hopefully. Then her thoughts drifted back to the missing book.

How could she tell her parents the truth?

Don't miss any of Mandie Shaw's
page-turning mysteries!

And look for the next book, coming soon!

The Missing Book

Lois Gladys Leppard

BANTAM BOOKS

NEW YORK • TORONTO • LONDON • SYDNEY • AUCKLAND

RL 2.6, ages 7–10
THE MISSING BOOK
A Bantam Skylark Book/March 2002

Mandie® and A Young Mandie Mystery® are registered
trademarks of Lois Gladys Leppard.

ISBN: 0-553-48718-3

Visit us on the Web! www.randomhouse.com/kids

Educators and librarians, for a variety of teaching tools,
visit us at www.randomhouse.com/teachers

Published simultaneously in the United States and Canada

BANTAM SKYLARK is an imprint of Random House Children's Books, a division of
Random House, Inc. SKYLARK BOOK and colophon and BANTAM BOOKS and
colophon are registered trademarks of Random House, Inc. Bantam Books, 1540
Broadway, New York, New York 10036.

PRINTED IN THE UNITED STATES OF AMERICA

OPM 10 9 8 7 6 5 4 3 2 1

With love to
Julia Elizabeth Maron,
Margaret and Joe Maron's Little Princess

1

Where Is It?

"LET'S SEE NOW," Mandie said to herself as she placed her books on a table in the parlor. "I think I'll do my reading assignment first."

Mandie had come home from school that March afternoon and had immediately sat down to begin her homework. Her mother was at Miss Abigail's house helping the neighbor women finish some needlework for Mrs. Chapman. Her father was outside working on the split-rail fence around their property. And her sister, Irene, was nowhere to be found.

Mandie shuffled through the books, looking for her reading book. It was not there.

"Oh, shucks!" she exclaimed. "I don't have my book. I wonder where it is." She thought for a moment and then said aloud, "Joe must have it. He must have forgotten to give it to me when he carried my books home from school."

The nine-year-old girl pushed back her long blond braid and tried to figure out how she could get her reading assignment done without the book. She couldn't borrow Irene's; her sister was two years older and did not have the same book.

At that moment Mandie's yellow cat, Windy, came in from the kitchen and began purring and rubbing around her ankles. Mandie picked her up. "Lucky you, you don't have such things as homework," she said to the cat, rubbing her head.

Mandie had never failed to do her homework, and this problem had her worried. Maybe she could go over to Miss Abigail's house and read her lesson out of Faith's book. Faith and her grandmother, Mrs. Chapman, were still staying with Miss Abigail because their house had not been completely repaired yet because of bad weather. But how would she get over there?

"I'll go ask my father if he will take me," Mandie said to herself. She quickly set the cat down. "You can't go, but I won't be gone long," she told Windy.

Windy looked up at her and let out a loud purr.

Mandie went to the front door, looked back to be sure Windy was not following her outside, and quickly slipped out. She hurried around the yard, searching for her father. She hadn't seen him when she came home, so she guessed he was at the back of the property.

Spring of 1898 was coming early in western North Carolina, and Mandie happily breathed in the fresh, warm air. Soon Charley Gap would be budding out all over with new leaves, and wildflowers would begin appearing in the woods. Mandie had hated wearing all her heavy winter clothes during the terribly cold winter they had had. Today was warm enough for her to come outside without her coat.

"Daddy, where are you?" Mandie yelled. She hurried toward the back property line.

Just as she passed the barn, her father suddenly appeared in the doorway. "Here I am," he called back to her.

"Oh, Daddy, I didn't even think about you being in the barn," Mandie said as she walked over to him.

"I'm repairing a harness," Mr. Shaw told her. "What was the rush all about?"

"I don't have my reading book and I need to do my homework so I was wondering if you would take me over to Miss Abigail's so I could use Faith's," Mandie quickly explained in one long breath.

"If you had homework in it, why didn't you bring it home?" her father asked.

"I thought I did—I mean, I was supposed to,

but somehow I don't have it," she explained. "Either Joe didn't give it to me with my other books when I came home or I left it at school. But I think I remember putting it in my stack to bring home, so most likely Joe has it."

"And you want to go to Miss Abigail's just to use Faith's book?" he asked.

"Yes, sir. You see, Mama is over there and I can come back home with her if you will take me now," Mandie told him.

"I'm sorry, Amanda, but it's not possible right now for me to take you," Mr. Shaw said, holding up a leather strap. "Your mother took the cart and I am repairing the other harness, so we can't use the wagon."

"Oh, shucks! What am I going to do?" Mandie said, blowing out her breath.

"Maybe you'll have time to read your lesson tomorrow before your class begins," her father suggested.

"I might," Mandie said, disappointed. "I'll be up on the road waiting when Joe comes by in the morning. If we hurry maybe I'll get to school early enough."

Mr. Shaw's blue eyes smiled down at Mandie's blue ones as he said, "And if you don't get it read in time, I'm sure Mr. Tallant will forgive you if you explain." He reached to push back a lock of his red hair as the wind ruffled it.

"Oh, if Joe has it, why didn't he bring it back to me? He knows I have homework," Mandie said with a loud groan.

"Maybe he will yet. You just got home," her father reminded her. "Go get the rest of your homework done just in case Joe does bring the book."

"Yes, sir, I suppose I'd better," Mandie replied.

She returned to the house and quickly did her other homework, still hoping Joe would come by. But by bedtime that night Joe had not shown up.

The next morning Mandie was up early and rushed through breakfast. She had been up at the road waiting for Joe for at least thirty minutes before he finally came.

Mandie hurried to meet him. "I was hoping you'd come by early," she told him as he reached to take her books. He always carried her books to school and then home in the afternoon.

"Early? Why?" Joe asked as Mandie started down the road.

"I don't have my reading book and couldn't do my homework. Do you have it?" Mandie asked, looking up at him as her short legs tried to keep up with his long ones.

"Your reading book? No, I don't have your reading book," he replied.

"Didn't I give it to you with all my other books when we left school yesterday?" Mandie asked.

"Why, no," Joe said. "I gave you all the books you gave me."

Mandie blew out her breath. "Then I must have left it at school, because I didn't have it when I got home."

"Yes, it must be at school," Joe agreed.

When they got to the schoolhouse, they found they were early after all. Mr. Tallant, the schoolmaster, was at his desk, but the only other pupil there was Faith.

"Good morning. Y'all are early too," Faith greeted them as Mandie hurried down to her desk.

"Yes, I'm looking for my reading book," Mandie told her. She quickly went through the books in her desk. "It's not here." She looked over at Joe.

He shrugged. "I'm sorry, but I have no idea where it is."

Mandie explained her dilemma to Faith, who immediately held out her reading book. "Here, use mine," she said. "You've got time to read the assignment before we begin class."

"Thank you," Mandie said gratefully, taking the book and quickly turning to the appropriate page.

By the time all the other pupils had arrived, Mandie was finished with the lesson and gave the book back to Faith. Now she was prepared for today. But what would she do about homework for tomorrow?

And where was her reading book? What had happened to it? It had to be somewhere, but where?

When school was out for the day, Faith again came to the rescue. "Mandie, why don't you come home with me and do the assignment in reading out of my book?" she said as she left the schoolhouse with Mandie and Joe. "Your mother is there again today working on the needlework. You could go home with her."

"That's a good idea, except my father will be wondering where I am if I don't get home on time," Mandie told her.

"I could go by your house and tell him," Joe offered as the three started down the road.

Mandie stopped to look up at the tall boy. "Would you, Joe?" she asked.

"Sure," Joe replied. "You girls go ahead. I'm going to take the shortcut." He started off toward the woods.

"Wait!" Mandie called. She ran to catch up with him. "Joe, how about not mentioning the book? Just tell my father I went home with Faith and will come back with my mother. You see, I haven't decided what to tell them about the book." Her parents wouldn't be happy to hear she had lost a schoolbook.

"All right," Joe agreed. "See you in the morning."

"Thank you, Joe," Mandie called back to him as she went to join Faith.

"It is strange about your book, isn't it? It seems to have just vanished," Faith remarked as they walked on.

"Yes, I can't figure it out at all," Mandie said, frowning. "I've been wondering if maybe Joe could have dropped it on the way to my house from school yesterday. Of course, I won't say that to him because he wouldn't like it."

"But, Mandie, if he had dropped it I'd think someone would have found it," Faith replied.

"Yes, and my name is on the first page inside the book," Mandie said. "There is also an inkblot from it that just barely smudged a place on the top edges of the pages. You can barely see it, but I know it's there."

"Wouldn't you think if someone found it they'd return it to you?" Faith asked.

"Some animal could have found it and carried it off somewhere," Mandie said, her eyes wide.

Faith's eyes widened too.

When Mandie and Faith got to Miss Abigail's house, they found Mandie's mother sitting in the parlor with Miss Abigail, Mrs. Chapman, and several other ladies. All were busily doing needlework.

Mrs. Shaw looked up at Mandie in surprise. "Is something wrong, Amanda?"

Mandie smiled and said, "Oh, no, Mama. I decided to walk home with Faith so we could do our homework together while you are here."

"Well, then you'd better get at it," Mrs. Shaw told her. "I don't plan on staying much longer."

"Yes, ma'am," Mandie replied.

"Come on, Mandie, let's go up to my room," Faith said, leading the way into the long hallway and toward the staircase.

Once they were behind closed doors in Faith's room, Faith handed her reading book to Mandie. "Here, do this first."

"Thank you," Mandie said, accepting the book

and turning the pages to find the homework assignment.

Before long Mandie was finished, and once again she and Faith discussed the missing-book situation.

"What are you going to do?" Faith asked. "You are welcome to use my book anytime, but you do need your own book."

"I don't really know what to do," Mandie replied, sitting on the window seat overlooking the front yard. "Our books cost so much money now. I remember my mother and father talking about it back at the first of this school year. It seems the books keep going up in price every year, and I know my parents don't have a lot of money. And they might think I was just careless and lost it."

"But I think they would want to be sure you had the necessary books to learn your lessons," Faith said. "I think you ought to tell them."

"I suppose I'll have to sooner or later. We have a lot of school time left yet before we get out for the summer," Mandie said with a big sigh. "I'd like to find my book. I thought maybe I could search for it awhile longer before I tell them it's missing."

"I'll help you all I can, Mandie," Faith offered.

"I just don't know how to begin looking for it," Mandie said. "I don't know when it disappeared. Before I went home from school? Or did it get lost on the way home, or what? I do know I had it that morning at school. I definitely know that."

"Do you think another pupil could have borrowed it that day? Without you seeing them, that is?" Faith asked.

"I don't know how anyone could have done that without my seeing them," Mandie said.

"You will have to tell Mr. Tallant you don't have your reading book, because he asks us to read in class a lot," Faith reminded her.

"I know," Mandie said as she stood up. "Let's go back downstairs. My mother may be getting ready to go home."

When the girls returned to the parlor, the ladies had paused in their needlework and were listening to Mrs. Chapman's latest news. Faith's grandmother had had medical treatment in New York back in the winter for burns on her face and was now in much better health. She was looking for a teaching position; she had been a schoolteacher before the accident.

Mandie and Faith quietly slipped into chairs at the rear of the room and listened.

"After applying at so many places, I finally received this letter just today from the school board in

Tellico asking that I come out for a personal interview," Mrs. Chapman was saying. She smiled and added, "I have already replied that I would be glad to receive an appointment date from them."

"That is so wonderful, that you can get back into your profession," Mrs. Woodard was saying.

Mandie quickly realized she would lose her dear friend Faith if her grandmother accepted a position over in Tellico. They would be moving. Mandie knew Mrs. Chapman needed to go back to work, but she secretly hoped it would not happen yet.

"Oh, Faith!" Mandie exclaimed, looking at her friend.

To her surprise, Faith smiled and said, "Yes, isn't that good news? My grandmother thought she would never be able to teach again because of the damage the fire did her face, but thanks to Dr. Woodard for taking her to those New York doctors, she is better enough to work again."

Mandie made herself smile. "Yes, Faith, that is good news for her." She wouldn't meet Faith's eyes.

Mrs. Shaw stood up. "Time to go home, Amanda," she said.

The other ladies also rose and agreed it was time for them all to go home for the day.

"Yes, ma'am," Mandie replied, glancing at

Faith. "Thanks for letting me use your book. I'll decide what to do about mine and let you know."

"Until you get another one, you are welcome to share mine," Faith said.

On the way home with her mother in the cart, Mandie thought about her book and tried to decide exactly what to do about it. She definitely would have to get another book, but she couldn't settle on how to go about it.

"Amanda, why so quiet?" her mother asked as they drove along the trail.

"Oh, I was just thinking," Mandie replied.

"Thinking about what?"

"Mrs. Chapman taking a job way off somewhere. Faith would have to move away," Mandie said.

"I know it's hard to lose a friend, but just think what this will do for Mrs. Chapman if she is able to secure the position," Mrs. Shaw said. "She will be able to earn a living for herself and Faith. And after losing all her family in that fire back in Missouri, she has no one but Faith. She needs Faith worse than we need her."

Mandie looked up at her mother. "I know, Mama. I'm glad for Mrs. Chapman, and Faith seems to be glad about it too, even though she knows she will have to move."

"Don't worry about losing a friend. You and Faith can always visit, and you will make more friends in the future," Mrs. Shaw promised.

"Maybe someone will move into their old house if they leave here," Mandie said hopefully. Then her thoughts drifted back to the missing book.

How could she tell her parents the truth?

2
Decision Delayed

THE NEXT MORNING Mandie once again got to the road before Joe came along. She was anxious to tell him that Mrs. Chapman was applying for a teaching position all the way over in Tellico, Tennessee, and that if Mrs. Chapman was hired, she and Faith would be moving.

When Joe finally came down the road, she hurried to meet him.

"What's the hurry?" Joe asked, reaching to take her books.

"Oh, something terrible may happen soon, Joe. I thought about it all night," Mandie said in one long breath as she tried to keep up with him.

"About your book?" Joe asked, looking down at her.

"Well, I haven't found the book yet, but this is about Faith and her grandmother." Mandie explained about Mrs. Chapman's prospective job. "I don't want Faith to move away," she added.

Joe frowned. "Yes, but it would be for their good if Mrs. Chapman can go back to teaching—"

"I know, I know," Mandie interrupted. "But I was hoping her grandmother could find a job closer and they wouldn't *have* to move."

"Mandie, there aren't any schools near here, just ours," Joe reminded her.

"Maybe she could help Mr. Tallant teach," Mandie said. "Or maybe he will take a long vacation, or . . . something."

Joe shook his head. "I don't remember Mr. Tallant ever taking a vacation while school is in session."

"But if he had someone like Mrs. Chapman to fill in for him, he could take a vacation if he wanted to," Mandie argued.

Joe glanced at Mandie's books. "So, you haven't found your reading book yet."

Mandie sighed. "No."

"What are you going to do about it?" Joe asked.

"I haven't figured that out," Mandie said.

"If you're going to keep learning, you're going to have to have another book. Have you told your parents?" Joe asked, slowing down so Mandie wouldn't have to walk so fast.

Mandie shook her head. "I keep hoping I'll find it somewhere."

"What are you going to tell Mr. Tallant if he asks you to read in class?" Joe asked.

"I don't know. Just whatever I can think of," Mandie mumbled.

They turned down the lane to the schoolhouse. Mandie noticed that her sister, Irene, was already there and was sitting on a log with Tommy Lester. They both had their schoolbooks open. Mandie wondered how Irene could have made it to the schoolhouse before them; she had still been at home when Mandie left. *Oh, she took the shortcut through the woods with Tommy.* Irene was afraid to go into the woods alone.

"Looks like your sister and Tommy are doing their reading lesson out here," Joe remarked.

"Yes, Irene never does homework when she's supposed to," Mandie said. "At least I got mine done with Faith yesterday."

Joe looked at Mandie. "Does Irene have the same reading book you do?" he asked.

"No, but Tommy Lester does," Mandie replied. "He's the same age as Irene but he failed some of his classes."

At that moment Faith rushed up to join Mandie and Joe. The three entered the front door of the schoolhouse.

"Do you need to look at my book before class begins?" Faith asked as they hung up their coats by the door.

"No, thanks, Faith, but I still don't have my book," Mandie said as everyone went to their desks.

"You can use mine if Mr. Tallant asks you to read aloud today," Faith said.

"Thank you, Faith," Mandie answered.

Later Mr. Tallant did ask Mandie to read to the class. Flustered, Mandie looked across at her sister, knowing Irene would repeat whatever she said to their parents. "I'm sorry, Mr. Tallant, I don't have my book," Mandie finally replied.

Mr. Tallant smiled. "Let's not make a habit of forgetting our books, now." He looked around the room. "Amanda, will you join Esther and read from her book? Esther, will you please share?"

"Yes, sir," Esther replied with a frown.

"Yes, Mr. Tallant," Mandie said, standing up and stepping over to Esther's desk. Esther handed her reading book to Mandie, and Mandie continued standing as she read. Out of the corner of her eye, she could see Irene watching her. Her sister would probably tell her parents that she had forgotten her book, and she would have to give a long explanation.

When recess finally came, Mandie, Faith, and Joe ate their lunch outside.

"Mandie, my grandmother said I could go home with you from school if you'd like, because Miss Abigail and some of the other ladies will be at your house this afternoon working on the needlework. I can go home when she goes," Faith said, biting into the ham biscuit from her lunch pail.

"Oh, I'm so glad," Mandie said with a big smile as she pulled food from her pail. "We can do our homework together."

"Yes, and you can use my reading book," Faith replied.

"What are you going to do when a day comes up that you and Faith can't get together to share her book?" Joe asked.

"I can always share my book," Faith quickly said.

"I suppose I'll have to tell my parents that my book is missing," Mandie said, looking at the biscuit she had taken from her pail. The very thought of talking to her parents about the book made her lose her appetite.

After school the three of them walked down the

road toward Mandie's house. Irene caught up with them. "So you've lost your reading book. Mama and Daddy aren't going to like that." She snickered and ran on ahead.

"Never mind her teasing, Mandie," Joe said as he looked down at Mandie. "It's just important that you tell your parents about the missing book, because you do have to have another one."

Faith tossed back her long dark hair. "You might as well tell them."

Mandie felt sudden tears forming in her eyes. She blinked and looked ahead across the top of the Nantahala Mountains. "I know," she murmured, afraid Irene would tell. "I'll tell them."

That night at the supper table, Mandie finally got up the nerve. But just as she opened her mouth to speak, her sister asked a question.

"Mama, when are we going to the store to buy material for our spring clothes?" Irene asked.

Mandie blew out her breath and took a sip of water from her glass.

Mrs. Shaw looked across the table at Mr. Shaw. "Irene, money is tight right now. We'll just have to fix over the dresses you and Amanda wore last year. We can spruce them up with some new frills and let out the hems. They'll look nice."

"Oh, Mama, we won't be getting new dresses?" Irene asked, disappointment in her voice.

Mr. Shaw spoke then. "You heard what your mother said, Irene. The world doesn't hang on you girls getting new dresses every summer. Maybe later in the year we can buy something new. Right now we can't afford it."

"Yes, sir," Irene answered, and laid down her fork as she frowned.

"I understand, Daddy," Mandie said in a soft voice, relieved that Irene had not yet told them about the missing book.

"With the weather warming up all of a sudden, I think we'd better get started on the dresses this weekend," Mrs. Shaw said.

"Yes, ma'am," Mandie said.

Irene sat there silently toying with the food on her plate. Mandie kept holding her breath, hoping her sister would not bring up the subject of her reading book.

Finally supper was finished, the table cleared, the dishes washed, and everyone settled down for the evening. Irene took a book and said she was going upstairs to read. Mandie helped her mother roll the skeins of knitting yarn into balls while her father sat by the fireplace reading. Everyone was unusually quiet. Even Windy was subdued, now and then reaching for a length of yarn.

"You do understand about your summer clothes, don't you?" Mandie's mother asked. "It's not that we don't want you and Irene to have new clothes. We wish you could. But we'll just have to wait for a while."

"Don't worry about it, Mama," Mandie said. "It doesn't matter to me."

Mr. Shaw looked up from his book and cleared his throat. "When you girls get older you'll understand. We have to put the most important things first when it comes to spending our money."

"It's all right, Daddy. I don't care if I don't get a new dress all summer," Mandie said, wishing her parents would stop talking about money. "Lots of our friends let out their dresses."

Mandie tried to change the subject. "Did Mrs. Chapman have anything else to say about her application to that school over in Tennessee?" she asked.

"No, I didn't see Mrs. Chapman today," her mother said. "She had other things to do, so she didn't come with the other ladies. Besides, it's too soon to get a reply back about that appointment."

"I'm so anxious to know what they will be doing . . . whether they will move away or not," Mandie said.

"I believe we have enough rolled for now," Mrs. Shaw told her as she finished rolling the last ball of yarn.

Mr. Shaw closed his book, stood up, and stretched. "Time to get some rest. The men are supposed to meet about six o'clock in the morning over at Mrs. Chapman's to see if we can get some work done on the house."

Mandie looked at him and said, "Six o'clock? That early?"

Mr. Shaw smiled. "Yes, that early. We'll have to quit around noontime so we can get our own chores done."

Mandie rose and took a book from the shelf by the fireplace. "I'm not sleepy. I'll sit in the kitchen awhile and read."

"Just don't stay up too late now, Amanda," Mrs. Shaw told her as she placed her knitting materials in the basket by her chair.

"Yes, ma'am," Mandie said, going into the kitchen and closing the door.

She sat down near the cookstove. Its warmth felt good now that nighttime had come with its cooler temperatures. Propping her feet on the woodbox, she opened the book. But she didn't even see the pages before her. Instead, she tried to figure out where she should look for her book. The house wasn't very big, so there was not a large area to search. She waited until her parents had gone to bed and then quietly stood up and looked around.

"I'll search the kitchen and the pantry tonight," she whispered to herself. "And tomorrow I'll search our room upstairs while Irene is out."

To Mandie's annoyance, Windy seemed to think her mistress was playing games with her and followed Mandie around the room, loudly purring and meowing. Mandie opened cupboards, drawers, and bins. She stopped to look under everything and examined the shelves in the pantry. Finally she finished, with no luck. She had not really expected to find her book in the kitchen.

With a deep sigh, Mandie sat down again and looked at the book she was supposed to be reading. She decided to read a little of it so she would not have been telling an untruth when she said she was going to read.

Her mind wandered. This missing book was a very peculiar mystery. She couldn't figure out a single clue as to how or when the book had disappeared.

She tried to think back and remember every little detail of the day when she had first missed it, which was Monday. She remembered bringing the book home on Friday before that, because she'd had homework in it. She should have taken it back to school with her on Monday, but she couldn't remember whether she had or not. There had been no reading in class on Monday, but Mr. Tallant had assigned a reading lesson for the next day. Therefore, she should have brought the book home with her on Monday, but it had not been with her other books when she got home that afternoon.

"Oh, this is absolutely mind-boggling!" Mandie exclaimed to herself. Windy jumped into her lap. Mandie rubbed the cat's soft fur.

Then Mandie thought about her other problem. How was she ever going to tell her parents about the missing book when they had said money was tight?

And there was another important thing in her life. Would Mrs. Chapman get the teaching position, accept it, and move away?

She couldn't sit up thinking about all this all night. She had to get some sleep. Closing the book, she set Windy down on the floor. "It's bedtime, Windy. Let's go."

Mandie quietly climbed the ladder to the upstairs room she shared with her sister. Windy, who had become an expert at going up and down ladders, followed.

"Maybe I'll dream up a solution to all this," Mandie mumbled as she prepared for bed.

3

More Questions

"JOE, I DO BELIEVE you have a secret," Mandie teased as they walked down the road the next morning. She smiled up at him. He grinned back without replying. He seemed awfully happy about something.

"Well, what is it? Joe, tell me," Mandie begged.

"What are you talking about, Mandie?" Joe asked, still grinning.

"You seem all excited and I want to know why," Mandie replied, pausing to stomp her foot.

"Now wait, Miss Amanda Elizabeth Shaw, I don't have to tell you all my business," Joe said, trying to act serious.

"Joe, tell me, please," Mandie insisted as they walked on. "I promise not to tell anyone else your secret."

"Well, you can't, because I just don't have a secret," Joe answered. "Come on now, Mandie, or we'll be late for school."

Mandie walked faster as he hurried on.

"All right then, I won't ever tell you any more of my secrets if you are not going to tell me yours," Mandie said as they turned down the lane to the schoolhouse.

"Come on, Mandie," Joe called back to her as he stepped up on the front porch.

Mandie followed as he opened the door. They were the first pupils there. Mr. Tallant was at his desk. "Good morning," he said, then went back to his work.

Joe walked down the aisle, laid Mandie's books on her desk, and went across the room to his seat.

As Mandie sat down, other pupils began coming into the room. Soon everyone was present and Mr. Tallant called the roll.

"Your assignment is to solve the problems on pages thirty-two and thirty-three," the schoolmaster told Mandie's group. He gave instructions for classwork to each of the other three groups.

Mandie's arithmetic book happened to be on top of her stack of books. Opening it, she began to work. She glanced up now and then and saw Joe smiling at her across the room. It was hard to keep her mind on the assignment. What was Joe's secret? And how could she get him to tell her what it was?

At the noon recess Faith ate with Mandie and Joe.

She and her grandmother had been discussing the possibility of their moving to Tellico, and Faith was excited about it.

"Oh, I do hope my grandmother is given the job," Faith told them. "She seems happy for the first time since the fire."

"I'm glad she is better now and can go back to teaching," Joe said.

Mandie silently chewed her biscuit and wouldn't look directly at Faith. She was secretly hoping they wouldn't move.

"My father and the other men in the neighborhood went over to your grandmother's house about six o'clock this morning to do some work on it," Mandie said, trying to change the subject. "He said now that the weather is better they will probably get everything done soon."

"Yes, my grandmother has been so grateful to all the people here in Charley Gap. They've been real neighbors," Faith said. "Yet if my grandmother gets that teaching position we probably won't even move back into our house. Miss Abigail said there would be no sense moving in there for a little while and then moving on to Tellico."

"That would be a lot of unnecessary trouble," Joe agreed, eating his sausage biscuit.

"Oh, I forgot to mention," Faith said, suddenly excited. "Have y'all heard about the person Mrs. Clifton saw in our yard over there after dark?" Mrs. Clifton helped Mrs. Chapman with her needlework. She lived close by.

"A man or a woman?" Mandie asked.

"Mrs. Clifton said it was either a tall, slender man, or maybe a woman. It's always too dark for her to tell," Faith explained.

"What are they doing when she sees them?" Mandie asked, anxiously leaning forward.

"She said it looked to her like they were just walking around the house and looking in a window now and then," Faith said, swallowing the last bite of her pound cake.

"We could all go over and sit and watch one night," Joe suggested.

"My grandmother said maybe it was just someone traveling through," Faith told them. "But Mrs. Clifton said she has seen this person several different nights. If they were just traveling through they would continue on. They seem to be just hanging around."

"Then why don't we go watch for them one night?" Mandie asked.

Faith shook her head. "It might be dangerous."

"I will speak to my father about it," Joe said, rising from the log where they had been sitting.

"And I will mention it to my father," Mandie added.

"And right now it's time to go back inside," Faith told them.

"I'll ask my father if he and the men saw anything wrong over there today," Mandie said as the three followed the other pupils back into the schoolhouse.

After recess Mr. Tallant collected the papers from all the morning assignments. "I'm going to give all of you an easy assignment for homework, which you can begin now," he announced, pausing to look around the room.

Mandie smiled. This was very unusual.

"I want all of you, every group, to write a poem," the schoolmaster explained. "Have the poems finished when you arrive at school tomorrow. Then we will read the poems in class and discuss them."

"Oh, no!" was heard from several pupils.

Mr. Tallant smiled and said, "Now, I know all of you aren't poets, but at least make an effort to write something. We'll vote on what you write, and whoever has the winning poem will be made class poet."

This was something new. A buzz went around the

room. Mandie saw Joe raise his hand, and when Mr. Tallant acknowledged him, Joe asked, "Is there a certain subject we must write about, sir?"

Mr. Tallant replied, "No, I'll just leave the subject open. In fact, write about anything, at any length. You may all begin now. I will take the papers in the morning. Be sure you have your poem ready when you arrive at school tomorrow."

There was a rustle as everyone opened their tablets to begin. Then silence fell over the room, with a sigh here and there.

Mandie glanced at Joe. He was hastily scribbling. Faith was looking at her and smiling. Mandie smiled back and shrugged. She didn't know what to write about. She had been writing poems ever since she had learned to read and write, but her poetry was private, and she had never allowed anyone to see the poems or even to know about them. She kept them in a box under her bed. And now whatever she wrote would be made public. It would have to be something that was not personal.

"Hmmm," she said under her breath. "Maybe a poem about Windy." She thought about that for a moment. "Or about the snow we've had this winter. Or . . ." She was out of possibilities.

Maybe when she got home she would be able to think better.

Joe seemed to be having no problem as he hurriedly scribbled away. Mandie noticed that Faith was writing something very slowly. Her other classmates were bent over their tablets.

Mandie was surprised when the school bell rang for dismissal. Glancing at the big clock at the front of the schoolroom, she saw that it was indeed time to go home. Where had the afternoon gone?

On the way home Faith declared, "I can't decide what to write a poem about." Looking at Joe and Mandie, she asked, "Have y'all?"

Mandie waited to see what Joe's reply would be, but he just grinned at the two girls and kept walking.

"Well, I haven't either," Mandie told Faith. "I'll decide when I get home."

After Faith left them at the crossroads to continue on her way to Miss Abigail's house, Mandie tried to find out why Joe was being so secretive.

"Joe, please tell me your secret. Please?" she said, walking fast to keep up with him.

"Mandie, I told you I don't have a secret. There's no secret to talk about," Joe replied.

"Then why are you acting so happy today?" Mandie asked.

"What are you writing your poem about?" he asked instead of answering.

"What are *you* writing *your* poem about?" Mandie asked.

"I asked first," Joe reminded her, grinning as they continued down the road. "What are you writing about? Do you hope to become the first class poet?"

Mandie stomped her feet as she walked on. "I don't know what I'm going to write about right now. I haven't decided," she said. "And I am not interested in being class poet. Now, I answered your questions. Why don't you answer mine?"

"But I did, Mandie," Joe declared.

"No, you didn't," Mandie replied. "You didn't say what you are writing your poem about."

Joe ran his fingers through his brown hair as they continued down the road. "I can't really answer that because right now I am trying out several ideas and don't know which one I will settle on." He grinned down at her. "Now, does that settle your inquiry?"

"Will you let me know in the morning on the way to school what your poem is about?" Mandie persisted.

"Maybe," Joe said. "If you promise to tell me what yours is about."

"All right, then," Mandie answered, taking a deep breath as they came to the path leading to the Shaws' house. Joe handed her books to her.

"See you in the morning," he said, turning to go down the road.

"Don't forget to ask your father about someone being seen at Mrs. Chapman's house and all that," Mandie called to him.

"All right," Joe yelled back.

As she started on down toward her house, Mandie thought about a possible explanation for the person Mrs. Clifton had seen. Maybe Mandie's father had heard something about this. She looked down the pathway and smiled as she saw him working on the split-rail fence he was putting up around their property. She hurried forward to ask questions that he might be able to answer.

Then she remembered her missing book. That was a problem she did not wish to discuss with her father *or* her mother right now. She knew she would have to sooner or later if she didn't find the book, but just maybe it would turn up somewhere. She smiled as she realized she had not had a reading assignment in class or for homework. She had managed another day without her book.

Windy came running to meet her, and she stooped to pick up the cat. "Maybe I'll just write my poem about you, Windy." Mandie rubbed her cheek on the cat's fur, and Windy purred loudly.

Her father called to her. "Have a nice day at school?"

"Oh, yes, Daddy," Mandie replied, hurrying to his side. "We didn't do much today, and we don't even have any homework except to write a poem." Without taking a breath, she asked, "Daddy, have you seen anyone prowling around Mrs. Chapman's house?" She looked up at him, anxiously awaiting his reply.

"Someone prowling around Mrs. Chapman's house? No, I haven't. What makes you ask that?" Mr. Shaw asked, straightening up from his task.

Mandie explained about Mrs. Clifton's seeing someone there.

"Well now, I suppose some of us men should go back over there and check things out," Mr. Shaw replied. "We worked on the outside this morning. We didn't go inside the house."

"Daddy, please let me go with you, please," Mandie instantly begged.

"Not this time, Amanda," Mr. Shaw said. "I'll ride

the horse over to Lakey's house and we men will get together from there. I won't be taking the wagon." He began picking up his tools. "I'll need to get started right away, while it's still daylight."

Mandie was disappointed. "Will you tell me all about everything when you come back?" she asked.

"Of course, Amanda," her father replied. "Now, you run along into the house and tell your mother where I am going. That will save me a few minutes."

"Yes, sir," Mandie said, turning down the lane to the back door of the house. "Please hurry back," she called to him.

"Yes, ma'am," Mr. Shaw replied with a grin.

When Mandie stepped into the kitchen, she found her mother already preparing supper. Mandie set Windy down and took off her coat.

"Mama, I'm supposed to tell you that Daddy has gone to Mr. Lakey's house and will get all the men to go over to Mrs. Chapman's house," Mandie began explaining, and related the story about someone's being seen over there.

"Well now, I suppose he won't be gone long, so you just get in there and get your homework done and I'll get supper ready," Mrs. Shaw replied, checking the contents of a pot on the cookstove.

"Yes, ma'am," Mandie said, going to hang her coat on the peg by the parlor door.

She took her books into the parlor and sat down. Looking at the books, she mumbled, "Now, why did I bring all those books home when I don't have any homework in any of them?"

Mandie was frustrated with Joe. She was sure he was hiding a secret about something. And there was no way she could get him to discuss it.

She picked up her tablet from the pile of books and turned to a clean sheet. She definitely had to write a poem about something.

"Maybe I'll write one about Joe's secret. I could make up a secret that he just might have," she said thoughtfully. She grinned to herself. "And we will probably have to read these poems in class. What would he say then? Might be fun."

She settled down with her pencil and began.

4

Writing Poetry

THE NEXT MORNING when Joe went to take Mandie's books, she insisted on holding on to the tablet. That was where she had hidden her poem.

"No, I'll carry this," she said, handing her books to Joe and tightening her grasp on her tablet.

Joe looked at her in surprise. "Why don't you want me to take the tablet? I always carry everything for you."

"Well, not this time," Mandie replied, frowning as she tried to avoid his brown eyes. "It's not very heavy. I'll carry it."

"Hmmm!" Joe muttered. "You're afraid I'll look at your poem, aren't you? Because the poem is bound to be in that tablet." He grinned.

"Well . . . ," Mandie said slowly, "you are not offering to let me read your poem, so you can't read mine."

Joe started up the road. Mandie quickly followed.

"Just don't forget, you'll have to read it out loud in class where everyone will hear you," Joe reminded her.

"I know, but that will be different," Mandie said. Trying to change the subject, she asked, "Did you ask your father about the Chapman house? I asked my father and he and some of the men went over there to look around after I got home from school. They couldn't find any sign of anyone or anything wrong over there."

"My father said we should stay away from there until someone finds out about this person Mrs. Clifton has been seeing. And he was going to talk to your father and some of the neighborhood men who have been working on the old house," Joe told her. "He thought it could have been someone just passing through and stopping there to rest awhile."

"Maybe whoever it was has gone on and won't be back again," Mandie said, breathing in the crisp morning air. Part of her hoped the person was gone—but another part of her hoped not. Then there would be a mystery to solve!

"How long is your poem?" Joe asked as they continued down the road.

"Not very long," Mandie replied. If he wouldn't tell her what she wanted to know, she was not going to give him any details.

"Like a dozen lines or so?" Joe asked, looking down at her.

"Oh, no, not that many," Mandie answered. "It's short, so I won't have to take a lot of time reading it in class."

"So is mine," Joe finally admitted. "Even so, it's sure going to take a long time to get all our poems read and discussed."

Mandie shrugged. "I suppose so. We probably won't have time to do anything else in class. And I hope we won't have to use our reading books today."

"Because you haven't found your reading book yet, have you?" Joe asked.

"No, but I'm still looking," Mandie told him. "And before you ask me, I have not told my parents yet that it's missing."

"I'm surprised your sister has not told them," Joe remarked.

"I am too, but I suppose she has just not thought of it at the right time," Mandie said.

"Maybe you'll find it before Irene tells," Joe said.

"I have searched the kitchen and the pantry, and

as soon as I get a chance I'll search the upstairs," Mandie said.

As they came to the crossroads, Mandie saw Faith waiting at the intersection. She and Joe hurried to join her.

"I wanted to catch you to let you know I have permission to go to your house after school today," Faith told Mandie. "Miss Abigail will be there again with the other ladies working on needlework and I can go home with her."

"Oh, I'm so glad," Mandie replied as the three walked on down the road toward the schoolhouse.

"Have y'all got your poems ready?" Faith asked.

"All done," Joe said.

"I wrote mine, but I'm not sure I want to read it in class," Mandie admitted.

"Aha!" Joe exclaimed. "I knew you weren't very happy about writing the poem."

"I'm just not sure how it will sound when I read it out loud," Mandie said.

"I'm sure it will be fine. Why, most of our class probably doesn't know how to begin to write a poem. I think it's going to be a hilarious time," Faith said with a big smile.

And it did turn out to be a hilarious day at school. The pupils giggled and laughed and sometimes howled as the others read their poems. Mr. Tallant tried to keep silence in the room, but it was impossible, so he finally gave up.

Then it was Joe's turn to read his poem. Mandie straightened up to listen.

Joe cleared his throat and began. *"There's a particular lass in this class, with blond hair and skin fair—"*

Mandie quickly covered her ears as she felt her face turn red. *She* was the only one in the class with really blond hair. She tried to close out Joe's voice, but everyone had fallen silent to listen and she could hear a word now and then.

"And you can be sure she'll find a mystery here," Joe finished.

Everyone clapped, and Mandie put her hands over her face. It was embarrassing to have a poem written about you and then read aloud to your friends. She didn't like it at all.

Then she heard Mr. Tallant calling on her to read her poem. She had come prepared. She quickly flipped open her tablet, pushed the poem she had written about Joe between two blank pages, and took out another poem, this one about her cat. She had not been sure she would be able to stand up and read the poem about Joe. Now she was sure she would not.

"*Windy is my little yellow cat,*" Mandie began, standing before the class. "*The day was windy when I named her that, and like the wind she breezes in and out of the house, always looking for a mouse. Although our language we can't mend, she is my own trusted little friend.*"

The class howled, stomped, and clapped when she finished. Mandie smiled and sat down at her desk.

The reading of the poems and the discussions concerning them took up the whole day, and when time came for dismissal, Mr. Tallant stood up and told the class, "You have all done a good job at writing poetry, but we are not going to have time to vote on the class poet today. Since today is Friday, I want you all to think about the different poems read today and make your decision by Monday about which one you want to vote for. The writer of the winning poem will be made class poet. Now, have a nice weekend."

Everyone stood up, ready to rush outside. Loud conversations drifted about the room as some of the pupils discussed the poems. Mandie didn't want to hear her poem talked about, so she hurried to the door, grabbed her coat, and went outside. Faith and Joe followed her.

"That wasn't—" Joe began as the three walked down the road.

"I don't want to discuss it," Mandie interrupted. "Let's talk about something else." She turned to Faith. "Did your grandmother hear from the people in Tellico?"

Joe frowned as they walked on. Faith looked at Joe, smiled, and then answered, "No, Mandie, not yet. I don't think they've had time yet to reply."

"Maybe y'all won't have to move," Mandie said.

"But, Mandie, if my grandmother gets the job, we will. It's too far to travel over there and back every day. You know that," Faith reminded her.

Mandie sighed loudly. "I know. I just hate to see you move away."

"And I hate to move away and leave my friends here, but I'm glad for my grandmother's sake," Faith said. "If we do move, maybe you could spend a weekend now and then, and I could come over and spend a weekend at your house."

"And what about me? Can I come too?" Joe teased as he slowed down so the girls could keep up with him.

Faith laughed. "Of course, Joe, anytime."

"Come to think of it, I'm sure my father has some patients over at Tellico, since there is not a doctor near there that I know of," Joe said. "My father probably travels over there now and then." Turning to Mandie, he said, "You and I could go with him sometime."

"Oh, yes, that would be nice," Mandie agreed.

When the three arrived at the pathway to the Shaw house, Faith asked, "Joe, why don't you come on down to Mandie's house and do your homework with us? Your mother is probably here with the ladies doing needlework."

"I'll go on down to the house with y'all and see," Joe answered.

Mrs. Woodard was there in the parlor with Miss Abigail and Esther's mother, Mrs. Rogan. Esther had not come. Mrs. Shaw looked up when the three entered the room. "There are some chocolate cookies in the kitchen left from our tea, if you young people are interested," she said. "And a pot of coffee."

"Thank you, Mrs. Shaw," Joe replied, grinning.

"We are going to do our homework in the kitchen, and I'll take care of everything. Thank you, Mama," Mandie said, hanging her coat on a peg on the wall as Joe and Faith did likewise. Then the three started toward the kitchen door.

"Don't eat too many of those cookies, Joe. I'm

sure Mrs. Miller will have our supper ready when we get home, and we aren't staying much longer," Mrs. Woodard said.

"Yes, ma'am," Joe said.

After Mandie and her friends were settled around the table in the kitchen with their books and cookies and coffee, Faith offered Mandie her reading book. "Here, read the next assignment in here," she said. "I know you don't have your book, and this way you can be one day ahead of lessons."

Mandie took the book and opened it. "Thanks, Faith." She hesitated. "Do you think the school over in Tellico will have the same books we have here in our school?"

Faith looked surprised. "I don't know, Mandie. I suppose all schools in this area would have the same books."

"But that's over the line in Tennessee, and they might not," Joe said, looking from Faith to Mandie.

If Faith was not going to have the same books, maybe she would let Mandie have her reading book when she moved.

The three finished their homework just as the women finished their afternoon needlework and prepared to leave. Everyone was standing around in the kitchen talking.

Mandie turned to Faith. "Thank you for letting me use your book," she told Faith.

Mrs. Shaw heard the remark and asked, "Amanda, where is your book?"

Mandie blinked. "I don't have it right now, and—"

At that moment Irene rushed in through the back door. "Mama, can I go to Bryson City? Tommy Lester's mother and father are going to Bryson City next Saturday, and I want to go. May I, please?" She stood before her mother, waiting for a reply.

Mrs. Shaw frowned. "Irene, please calm down. As you see, we have other people visiting us here. Now, just why are Mr. and Mrs. Lester going to Bryson City?"

Irene shook her head. "I don't really know. Tommy just said they were going. Please, let me go with them."

Mandie decided she would like to go also. "And may I go too, Mother?" she asked.

Mrs. Woodard looked around the room and said, "My, my, all the young ones wanting to go to Bryson City. You too, I suppose, Joe?" She looked at her son.

Joe grinned. "Of course if everyone else is going I'd like to go too."

Then Miss Abigail looked at Faith, who was silently listening. "Are you not interested in this journey over to Bryson City, Faith?"

Faith smiled at her. "I'd rather go with them than be left behind for a weekend by myself."

"All right, all right, I'll speak to Mrs. Lester when I see her at church Sunday," Mrs. Shaw told them.

"Come on, let's go outside," Mandie said to her friends. They already had their coats on, and while the adults were getting prepared to leave, she would be safe from her mother's question.

Irene followed them outside. As they stood about the yard, she said, "I don't know how we are all going to ride over to Bryson City."

"I have an easy solution to that," Joe said. "My father could ask Mr. Miller to drive all of us over in the wagon. Mr. Miller usually doesn't do much work on Saturday anyway."

"And you really don't know why the Lesters are going to Bryson City?" Mandie asked her sister.

"Tha's what I said," Irene replied, pushing back her dark hair.

"What if they have relatives they are going to

visit over there?" Faith said. "And suppose they are planning to spend the night?"

"Then we probably can't go," Mandie said.

"I've never heard of any relatives of the Lesters living over that way," Joe said. "I believe their relatives are all in the other direction, toward Buncombe County and on beyond. That's where they came from when they moved here a couple of years ago."

"I suppose we'll have to wait and see what your mother finds out, Mandie, when she talks to Mrs. Lester," Faith said.

Irene shuffled her shoes around in the dirt. "I don't know why everyone all of a sudden wants to go to Bryson City with the Lesters just because I want to."

"That's because we're so isolated here in Charley Gap, Irene, that we take every opportunity to get away," Joe explained.

"It's a long, rough road," Irene reminded them.

Mandie didn't want to get into an argument with her sister—though she believed Irene was trying to start one. Instead, she asked, "Who do y'all think will win the class poet title?"

"I just don't know. There were several really good poems read," Faith said. "And lots of applause."

"But the applause was terrific for every poem. We can't judge the winner by that," Joe said.

"I have already decided whom I'm going to vote for," Mandie said.

"Remember, you are supposed to vote for the poem, not for the person," Irene cautioned.

"Of course I know that," Mandie told her.

The ladies came outside and prepared to leave, Mrs. Woodard and Mrs. Rogan with Joe, and Miss Abigail with Faith in her cart.

"I'll see you at church on Sunday. I hope Mrs. Lester is there so your mother can talk to her," Faith called back to Mandie.

"If she isn't we can always go by her house," Joe added as he drove his mother's cart.

Mandie turned to go inside again. Her mother and Irene had already gone through the back door.

Now, if she could just avoid her mother long enough for her mother to forget about her book, maybe her mother wouldn't think of it later. But still, Mandie was going to have to do something about it.

5

Poetry Secrets

THE NEXT MORNING Mandie woke to a chilly room. As she reached down to pull the quilt up around her, she saw that it was not daylight. Only a faint glimmer of sky was showing through the window. Apparently her father had not yet built up the fire in the cookstove in the kitchen, which warmed the whole house, especially the upstairs, because heat rose.

"I'll just wait for Daddy to warm up the house," Mandie said to herself. As she started to turn over she almost smashed Windy, who was nestled under the edge of the quilt.

"Meow!" the cat protested, jumping away.

Mandie reached for Windy and pulled her back under the covers. "It's too cold to get up yet," Mandie whispered.

Windy snuggled up beside her and went back to sleep. Mandie lay awake, thinking about the day's work ahead of her. Her mother had said they would work on last year's clothes to get them ready for summer, and Mandie was not enthusiastic about all that work. Maybe her mother would postpone the sewing, since the weather had turned cold again. After all, it was only March, and the Nantahala Mountains would not warm up until sometime in May.

The weather could still be cold next Saturday, the day when the Lesters would be going to Bryson City, and Mrs. Lester might cancel their journey until it was warmer. Then Mandie had another thought. If they didn't work on their summer clothes today, her mother might decide she and Irene would not be able to go with the Lesters next Saturday, because that would be an all-day trip with no time for anything else.

"Oh, shucks!" Mandie groaned to herself as she realized they would have to do the sewing today. She pulled the quilt over her head and went back to sleep.

The aroma of perking coffee woke her later. She quickly sat up to look at the window. It was daylight now, but there was no sign of the sun. "Must be cloudy," she mumbled to herself as she slipped out of bed and began dressing.

Windy sat up on the covers and began washing her face. Irene was still asleep.

Mandie hurried down the ladder and into the kitchen, where she found her father sitting at the table drinking coffee and going over some papers.

"Good morning, Daddy," Mandie greeted him. "Are you doing some paperwork?"

"Good morning, my little blue eyes," Mr. Shaw answered, shuffling through the papers. "No, not really. I'm just going over our list of what has been done at Mrs. Chapman's house and what else needs work over there."

"You men are almost finished with everything, aren't you?" Mandie asked, going to the stove, filling a cup with coffee, and coming back to the table.

"We're getting close. But take a look out the window," Mr. Shaw said.

Mandie looked outside. "Do you think it's going to rain?" she asked, coming back to the table and pulling out a chair.

"Rain? No, I don't think so. Those are snow clouds if I ever saw any," Mr. Shaw explained.

"Snow? But, Daddy, it's March," Mandie said in surprise.

"I know, but we have had some bad snowstorms in March, maybe not since you can remember," he told her. "And of course everything here in Charley Gap comes to a standstill when that happens."

"Oh, Daddy, I hope it's not going to snow," Mandie said, frowning as she sipped the hot coffee. "We're going to vote for the class poet Monday, and if it snows that bad we won't be able to get to school."

Mr. Shaw smiled at her. "Maybe it won't snow much after all. So your class is going to have a class poet. Where did Mr. Tallant get such an idea?"

Mandie smiled. "I'm not sure. We had to write a poem and read it in class yesterday, but we didn't have time to vote. Mr. Tallant said we would vote on Monday for the class poet."

"And are you hoping to get the title?" Mr. Shaw asked.

Mandie shrugged. "Oh, no, Daddy, I don't want to be class poet. I might have to keep on writing poems and reading them in class."

"And you wouldn't like to do that?" he asked.

"No, because I don't want anyone to read my poems," Mandie said, and then stopped. She had never told her father she wrote poems.

"So you write other poems too," her father said, looking at her closely.

Mandie dropped her gaze. She couldn't lie to her father. "Yes, sir," she said in a low voice, holding her coffee cup with both hands.

"Now, that is really interesting. You have never

let me know that you wrote poetry. Where are these other poems?" he asked.

Mandie cleared her throat. "They're not available right now."

Mr. Shaw laughed. "In other words, you have them hidden away somewhere, right?"

Mandie blew out her breath and finally looked at her father. "Oh, Daddy, they are just dumb little poems I write for myself every now and then, so I don't want anyone else to read them."

"I would like very much to read some of them, Amanda," Mr. Shaw said, taking a sip of coffee. "You see, when I was young I also used to write poetry."

"*You* used to write poetry, Daddy?" Mandie was astonished.

"A long, long time ago," he said, frowning thoughtfully.

"Could I read some of your poems, Daddy?" Mandie asked.

Mr. Shaw cleared his throat. "They're not available right now." He tried to be serious.

Mandie laughed. "Well, when they are available could I read some of them?"

"I suppose so, if I am allowed to read some of yours when *they* are available," Mr. Shaw replied.

Mandie started giggling, and Mr. Shaw burst

out laughing. And at that moment Mrs. Shaw came into the kitchen.

"My, my, what's so funny this early in the morning, and with snow on the way besides?" she asked as she took a cup down from the cupboard.

Mr. Shaw immediately stood up and reached for the cup. "Sit down. I'll get your coffee," he told her, going to the stove to fill the cup. When he looked at Mandie, she tried to send him a silent signal not to tell her mother about the poetry. He seemed to understand.

"You may be right about that snow coming," Mr. Shaw told Mrs. Shaw.

"Won't make much difference today. We've got all that sewing to do," Mrs. Shaw replied.

"Will we get it all done today?" Mandie asked.

"A big part of it, I suppose," Mrs. Shaw said. "With the days getting longer now, we can do some more on afternoons when you girls don't have much homework. Now, you run upstairs and wake your sister and I'll see about getting breakfast started." She stood up.

"Yes, ma'am," Mandie replied. She quickly left the room and climbed the ladder upstairs.

"Irene, wake up. Mama said for you to get up," Mandie told her sister as she reached to pat her legs under the covers.

Irene rolled away from her. "I'll get up in a little while." She turned over.

"Irene, it looks like it's going to snow," Mandie said.

Irene opened her eyes and sat up. "Snow? It's not going to snow." She stared out the window. "Is it?"

"Daddy thinks it might." Mandie started toward the ladder. "Now, don't go back to sleep. Mama is cooking breakfast." She looked back. Irene was still sitting there, looking out the window.

Mandie returned to the kitchen. "I woke her," she said.

"Now get the dishes down and set the table, Amanda," Mrs. Shaw said, filling a pot with water and setting it on the cookstove.

Mr. Shaw was rolling out the dough for biscuits on the cabinet top. Mandie was hoping he had not mentioned her poems to her mother. As she placed the plates on the table, her father glanced at her and winked. She smiled back, hoping that was the signal that he had not discussed their conversation with her mother.

After breakfast was over and the table was cleared, Mrs. Shaw told the girls to bring down some of their summer dresses from the closet upstairs. Then she measured the length of the dresses. Mandie had grown only a couple of inches since last summer, and the deep hems on her dresses could be let down. But Irene had grown at least six inches, and even after the hems had been ripped out, her dresses were too short.

"We'll just have to add a frill around the bottom of that one to make it long enough," Mrs. Shaw told Irene as she stood there in a pale blue cotton dress.

"A frill? Won't that look tacky?" Irene asked, frowning as she looked down at her skirt.

"No, because I'll put a ruffle around the neck to match it. Why, people will think you've got a new dress," Mrs. Shaw replied.

Mandie was busy ripping out the hem on one of her dresses.

"And, Amanda, we only need to let half of that hem down to make your dress long enough," Mrs. Shaw told her.

"I'm glad my dress had such a big hem," Mandie remarked, finally getting to the end of the ripping.

Mr. Shaw had been out to the barn. Now he came back into the kitchen, blowing on his hands. "It is getting cold out there but no sign of snow yet." He hung up his coat and hat on the peg by the back door.

"Well, maybe it won't come," Mrs. Shaw said, measuring a piece of material to make the ruffle for Irene's dress. "I thought you were going over to work on Mrs. Chapman's house this morning."

"We were supposed to, but John Knight is the one designated as the driver today, and he hasn't shown up yet," Mr. Shaw replied.

Mandie wanted to go with her father if he went to work on Mrs. Chapman's house, but she knew she would never be allowed to go today. All this ripping and sewing had to be done.

"He has a long way to come down that mountain, so he probably decided he'd better wait and see if it snows," Mrs. Shaw replied.

"Maybe so," Mr. Shaw agreed, and went to put more wood into the cookstove.

At that moment Mandie heard a wagon come into the backyard. She looked out the window and saw Mr. Lester and Tommy step down from the vehicle. "It's Mr. Lester and Tommy," she told her father, who was looking across the room. She noticed Irene's eyes lighting up.

Mr. Shaw hurried to open the back door and let them in. "Come in, come in. How about a cup of hot coffee?" he welcomed the visitors.

"That might thaw me out. It's cold out there,"

Mr. Lester said, removing his hat and turning to Mrs. Shaw. "Morning, ma'am."

"Good morning, Mr. Lester. Why didn't you bring Mrs. Lester with you?" Mrs. Shaw asked.

"She took one look out the window this morning, decided it was going to snow, and declared she was not going outside," Mr. Lester replied.

The men and Tommy sat down at the table with coffee.

"I haven't seen anything of John Knight yet," Mr. Shaw said.

"That's why I'm here," Mr. Lester replied. "One of his boys came down to the house this morning to say his pa is not feeling well and was afraid it might snow. Since I live nearer to the mountain than you other men, he asked me to inform you all."

"I suppose we should just forget about doing any work over there today. I don't believe there's any hurry now to get things finished. Mrs. Chapman more than likely will be moving to Tellico and won't even go back to live in the old house," Mr. Shaw said.

"Did she get the job?" Mandie asked.

"No, Amanda, she has to go for an interview next week, and then she'll know whether she got it or not," Mr. Lester explained. "I came by Miss Abigail's on the way over here and Mrs. Chapman had just received word to come for the interview."

"Oh," Mandie said in a disappointed voice.

"Maybe she'll get the job and then y'all won't have to finish the work on her house," Irene said, looking straight at Tommy, even though she was speaking to his father.

"I don't know about that," Mr. Lester said.

"No, Irene, there are things that still need to be done to keep the old house from deteriorating further," Mr. Shaw said. "We have lots more work to do whether Mrs. Chapman moves away or not."

"But if she moves away, what will happen to the house? Will it just stand there empty?" Mr. Lester asked. "I've been wondering about that."

"Maybe she'll sell it," Mr. Shaw suggested. "But in the shape it's in right now, it wouldn't bring much money."

Mandie listened to the conversation and felt she was going to lose her dear friend Faith. She had been hoping Mrs. Chapman wouldn't get the job, but if the school had asked her to come for an interview, they must be really interested in hiring her. And Faith was the only friend Mandie had who lived near her. There was Joe, of course, but he was a boy. Mandie had been so happy when Faith and her grandmother had come to live in the old Conley place.

"Amanda, finish pinning up that new hem," Mrs. Shaw told her, bringing her back to the present.

"Yes, ma'am," Mandie replied, folding up the material on the edge of the skirt of her summer dress. Then she remembered Mrs. Clifton's saying she had seen someone at the old house. "Have you heard of anyone being seen around Mrs. Chapman's house, Mr. Lester?"

"No, I haven't," Mr. Lester replied. Looking at Mr. Shaw, he added, "Mrs. Clifton declares she has seen someone there at night, but no one else has seen this person, so I'm wondering about that."

"Maybe she has," Mr. Shaw said. "Or maybe the lady's eyesight is not too good after dark."

Mr. Lester smiled. "That might explain it."

Mandie wasn't so sure. Mrs. Clifton's eyesight was good enough to do the dainty needlework for Mrs. Chapman. She was sure Mrs. Clifton had seen someone. And she was going to find out for herself if there really was someone prowling around Mrs. Chapman's house at night.

6

Plans Canceled

"MAMA, MR. LESTER didn't say any-thing about going to Bryson City," Mandie said as she pinned up the remaining narrow hem on her dress. Mr. Lester and Tommy had left with-out anyone even mentioning their planned journey.

"I know, Amanda," Mrs. Shaw replied, still working on the ruffle for Irene's dress. "If I remember rightly, Mr. Lester does not plan such things. It's Mrs. Lester I have to speak to."

Mandie frowned as she thought about that. Her parents shared everything. Evidently Mr. and Mrs. Lester did not. Mrs. Lester must be the boss.

"That's right," Irene said. "It's Mrs. Lester who is planning the Bryson City journey."

"And the weather may prevent them from go-ing," Mrs. Shaw said. "But I will speak to Mrs.

Lester at church tomorrow. Now, let's get these dresses finished."

Mandie kept watching all day, but it didn't snow. Though the clouds hovered low and thick, no moisture fell.

And no one else came visiting at the Shaws' house that day. The alterations on the two dresses were finished by suppertime. Mandie and Irene were both pleased with the results.

Everyone went to bed early that night. Mandie was not sleepy, and she tossed and turned so much that Windy jumped off of her bed and climbed onto the foot of Irene's bed. Mandie held her breath, waiting for her sister to yell at the cat, but there was no sound, and Mandie decided Irene was asleep. Maybe Windy would come back to her before Irene woke up the next morning.

"Oh, me, oh, my," Mandie muttered to herself. She pulled the quilt up closer around her shoulders as she thought about Mrs. Chapman going for the job interview. Mrs. Chapman had been a schoolteacher for many years before she and Faith had moved to Charley Gap, so Mandie believed she would get the position. And Faith would move away. Mandie wouldn't have a friend living anywhere near her except for Joe. All her schoolmates lived in the other direction from the schoolhouse, too far away to visit. She felt a little chill of sadness pass over her.

Maybe she and Faith and Joe could solve the mystery of the unknown visitor seen by Mrs. Clifton at Mrs. Chapman's old house before Faith left for her new home. That would give Mandie something to think about besides Faith's departure.

"There's always an answer to a mystery," she whispered to herself. All she had to do was figure out how she was going to solve this one. If the person was only seen at night, it wouldn't do any good to spy on the place in the daytime. On the other hand, she didn't know how she could get permission to go over there at night. In fact, she knew it was impossible.

Maybe she could spend the night with Faith. She could also share Faith's reading book while there. Then she would be prepared if Mr. Tallant again involved her in the reading lesson in class, which she knew was pretty likely.

If she stayed overnight with Faith, she might be able to persuade Faith to come out with her to the old house during the night to look for the person roaming around there.

Just as she was dropping off to sleep, Mandie

remembered Joe's refusal to tell her his secret—and she was sure he did have one.

Somehow she would find out what it was.

The next day was cloudy and cold again. Mandie was glad to see that it had not snowed, because they would be going to church and her mother would talk to Mrs. Lester about Bryson City.

As she turned away from the window to get dressed, she saw that Windy was still on Irene's bed, but luckily her sister was asleep. Mandie quietly swooped up the cat and set her down on her own bed. Windy protested loudly, jumped down, ran to the ladder, and went downstairs. About that time Irene opened her eyes and sat up.

"Did it snow?" Irene asked, looking toward the window.

"No, but it's still awfully cloudy, and it must be terribly cold out there," Mandie replied, hastily beginning to dress.

"So we will be going to church and Mama will be asking Mrs. Lester about the journey to Bryson City," Irene replied, tossing back the quilt and getting out of bed.

At that moment they heard a horse in the yard below. Mandie hurried to the window to look down. Whoever it was had gone on around to the back, out of view.

"Who would be coming to visit this early in the morning?" Mandie said, mostly to herself, as she quickly buttoned up her dress.

"There must be an emergency of some kind," Irene said, picking up her dress.

"Daddy is up, I know, because I can smell the coffee perking," Mandie said, tossing back her long braid and smoothing it down. "I'm going to see," she added, and went across the room to go down the ladder.

"I am too," Irene said, straightening her skirt as she followed close behind Mandie.

When Mandie stepped into the kitchen with Irene, she saw their father standing in the doorway talking to Dr. Woodard, who was out on the back porch.

"Just let me grab my coat and hat and I'll be right with you," Mr. Shaw was saying as he reached to take his things from the pegs by the door. As he turned he saw the girls. "Be right back," he told them, and quickly went out the door and closed it behind him.

Mandie hurried to the back window to look out. Dr. Woodard's buggy was in the driveway, and as she watched, the doctor and her father stepped up into the vehicle.

"I wonder where they are going," Irene said behind her.

"Looks to me like they're just going to sit there and talk," Mandie replied. "The reins are still looped over the tree limb."

The girls watched for at least ten minutes, but the two men didn't go anywhere. Then Mr. Shaw stepped down from the buggy, and Dr. Woodard drove off.

"Why didn't Dr. Woodard come in the house?" Mandie asked when her father returned.

Mr. Shaw hung up his coat and hat. "We had some business to discuss privately." He went over to the cookstove and added more wood to the fire.

"But, Daddy, he still could have come inside," Mandie said. "We wouldn't have interfered."

Mr. Shaw straightened up and smiled at Mandie. "I know. But it was private business just between the two of us. Now, let's get started on breakfast."

Mandie frowned but didn't say any more. She got the silverware out of the drawer.

"Must have been private doctor business. Who cares?" Irene mumbled under her breath as she went to the cupboard to get the dishes for breakfast.

Then Mrs. Shaw came into the kitchen. "That sure was a short visit," she said. "The doctor must have been in a hurry." She went to the stove to check the contents of the coffeepot. It was full.

"Yes, he was. I'll explain later," Mr. Shaw said, nodding toward Mandie and Irene.

Dr. Woodard's visit was not mentioned again. The Shaws had breakfast and got ready to go to church.

Though the day was cloudy and cold, almost everyone in the community came for the church service that morning. As the Shaws sat down, Mandie looked around for the Lesters. They weren't there. Maybe they were just a little late. As the sermon progressed, she decided they were not coming.

"Tommy and his family are not here," Irene whispered to Mandie.

Mrs. Shaw, sitting on the other side of Irene, touched Irene's shoulder and shook her head. The two girls straightened up and turned their attention to the preacher delivering the message.

The sermon ran overtime. The tall clock in the corner softly chimed twelve, and the preacher continued until it struck half past. When the congregation rose to sing the closing hymn, Mandie took advantage of the noise to whisper to her sister again.

"Did Tommy tell you they weren't coming to church today?" she asked.

Irene shook her head. "No, he said they would be here."

Mandie sang along with the crowd as she tried to figure out what had happened to the Lesters. She still didn't know whether or not she and Irene would be allowed to go to Bryson City with them.

As soon as the preacher said the benediction, the congregation began filing out of the church, chatting happily. Mandie also heard complaints here and there about the preacher going overtime, especially on such a cold, cloudy day.

On the way home, Mandie listened for any conversation between her parents that might explain the Lesters' absence, but their name was never mentioned.

Later, during dinner, Mrs. Shaw finally spoke about the Lesters. As she passed the food around the table, she looked at the girls. "You girls won't be going to Bryson City with the Lesters next weekend because they won't be making the journey over there anytime soon."

"Why, Mama?" Mandie asked.

"How do you know, Mama? They weren't even in church today for you to talk to them about it," Irene said.

Mrs. Shaw looked over at Mr. Shaw. He didn't say a word. She turned back to the girls. "Mrs. Lester has fallen ill."

"When did she get sick?" Mandie asked.

"Last night," Mrs. Shaw said. "Now finish up your food and let's get the table cleared off."

Mandie remembered Dr. Woodard's early-morning visit and decided he had been over at the Lesters' and had come by to tell her father and mother that Mrs. Lester was ill. But why had he and her parents acted so mysterious about everything?

Later in the day Dr. Woodard came by again, and this time Joe was with him. They came into the house, and Mrs. Shaw set out cake and coffee in the kitchen for the young people. Dr. Woodard and Mr. Shaw went on into the parlor.

"Now, don't eat too much of this cake or none of you will want any supper," Mrs. Shaw said as she placed the cake in the middle of the table and uncovered it.

Mandie and Irene got plates and cups from the cupboard.

"Thank you, Mrs. Shaw," Joe said with a big grin as she sliced a piece for him.

"Amanda, you and Irene get yours. I'm going in the parlor to sit with Dr. Woodard and your father," Mrs. Shaw said as she left the room.

"I suppose they don't want any," Mandie said as they filled their cups from the percolator on the stove.

Joe cleared his throat. "They want to talk in there so we can't hear what they say."

"That's what I was thinking too, Joe," Mandie said, frowning. "You probably know your father came by this morning and my father went outside to sit in Dr. Woodard's buggy to talk. He told us it was a private conversation."

"Hmmm," Joe said. "They probably didn't want to discuss everything in front of you."

"What do you mean?" Irene asked.

"Yes, exactly what do you mean?" Mandie added.

"Well," Joe replied hesitantly, "I'm not sure I should tell y'all."

That made Mandie really curious. "Joe Woodard, what is going on?" she asked.

"You see, since my father is the doctor around

here, I learn all kinds of things about everybody, and I'm not supposed to ever repeat any of it," he said, looking at Mandie and then at Irene.

"Now you have to explain, or—or I'll just take away your chocolate cake," Mandie said, reaching for his plate. But Joe was too quick and moved it out of her reach. "Joe, please tell us whatever it is that you know."

"Both of you promise not to let anyone know I told you?" Joe asked, looking from Mandie to Irene.

"I promise," Mandie said eagerly.

"I do too," Irene added.

At that moment Mrs. Shaw came back into the kitchen. "I just need to get coffee to take into the parlor," she explained as she carried the cups to the stove.

"I'll help you, Mama," Mandie offered, quickly rising and getting a serving tray from the cupboard.

Mrs. Shaw reached for the tray and placed the cups of coffee on it.

"Don't y'all want any chocolate cake?" Mandie asked as her mother started out of the room.

"No, not right now," Mrs. Shaw said, going through the doorway toward the parlor. Looking back, she added, "We might later, so don't eat it all up."

"We couldn't possibly eat all that cake," Mandie told her, giggling.

As soon as the door closed behind Mrs. Shaw, Joe said, "I'm glad she didn't catch me in the middle of what I was going to tell y'all."

"Oh, Joe, hurry up and explain," Mandie urged him.

Joe began talking in a low whisper. "As I said, since I am the doctor's son, I learn lots of things. What I was going to tell y'all was that Mrs. Lester had a baby last night—"

"Joe!" Mandie interrupted.

Both girls stared at him in astonishment. That topic was not discussed between boys and girls. It was considered improper.

"All right, if you don't want to know what happened, I won't tell y'all, but you said you did want to know," Joe replied, frowning at them.

"All right, we'll listen, you do the talking," Irene answered.

"Like I just said, Mrs. Lester had a baby last night and it died," Joe replied.

The two girls were shocked again.

"Why? Why did it die?" Mandie asked.

"My father said it came too early, wasn't supposed to get here until June, and this is just March," Joe said, his expression grim.

"Oh, how awful!" Mandie exclaimed, tears flooding her eyes.

"I didn't know Mrs. Lester was going to have a baby," Irene said. "Are you sure she did?"

"Yes, I am. My father discusses all his cases with my mother, and sometimes I hear the conversation," Joe replied. "And I heard everything about Mrs. Lester."

"That explains why the Lesters weren't at church," Mandie said.

"Tommy never told me a word about his mother going to have a baby," Irene said, frowning.

"Irene, it would not be proper for him to tell such things," Mandie reminded her.

"Now with all this happening, my father won't be able to take Mrs. Chapman to Tellico for her interview this week," Joe said.

"Your father was going to take her?" Mandie asked.

"Yes, he was going to visit some of his patients over there and had offered to take Mrs. Chapman and Faith along," Joe replied.

"Faith is going with her grandmother? She'll miss school if she does," Mandie said.

"Mrs. Chapman told my father she wanted Faith to see the place and to be satisfied that she would want to move over there, just in case she gets the job," Joe explained.

"Then how is Mrs. Chapman going if your father can't take them?" Mandie asked.

"I don't know yet," Joe said, finally swallowing a big mouthful of chocolate cake and washing it down with coffee.

Mandie thought for a moment. "Maybe my father could take her." Then she added with a grin, "And just maybe I could go with him."

"Amanda Shaw, you know Mama won't let you miss school like that," Irene reminded her.

"Well, I could always ask," Mandie said.

As soon as she got the right opportunity she would ask her father. She had never been to Tellico, and if she could go with them, she would know where her friend would be living in case Mrs. Chapman got the job. A small consolation for having her friend move away, but Mandie would take it.

7

Waiting

THE NEXT MORNING when Joe met Mandie at the road to walk to school, he had news.

"Did you ask your father about driving Mrs. Chapman and Faith to the interview?" he asked, taking Mandie's books to carry.

"No, I haven't had the right chance yet," Mandie replied.

"Well, you don't have to ask," Joe said as they walked down the road. "My father has asked Mr. Miller to take them, and he can also do some errands for my father while he is over there. They are leaving tomorrow, the interview is Wednesday, and they'll come back Thursday." Mr. Miller and his wife worked for Dr. Woodard and lived on his property.

"I suppose my father wouldn't have gone anyway," Mandie said, disappointed by the decision.

Faith was waiting for them at the crossroads. Mandie noticed that she was unusually excited.

"We're going to Tellico tomorrow," Faith told them.

"I know. Joe just told me," Mandie replied, feeling guilty that she could not be excited about this journey.

"I appreciate your father's allowing Mr. Miller to take us," Faith said to Joe as they walked on toward the schoolhouse.

"My father didn't think he could be away right now with Mrs. Lester still not doing very well."

"I felt so sad when my grandmother told me about the baby," Faith said. She tossed back her long dark hair.

"I suppose they will be having a funeral," Mandie said.

"They had a private service late yesterday after we left your house, Mandie," Joe said.

Irene caught up with them. "Who do you think is going to be the class poet?" she asked, falling in step.

"Not me. I don't want to be it," Mandie said.

"I'm guessing Joe will get it," Irene said, glancing at him.

"No, I don't want to be class poet either," Joe told her. "Maybe Faith."

"No, leave me out of that," Faith said. "We all have to vote, so who are y'all voting for?"

"I haven't decided yet," Mandie said.

"If none of us really wants to win it, then why don't we decide among us who to vote for?" Joe said.

"How about Esther?" Faith said. "I thought her poem was good. Remember, it was about the birds in her mother's flower garden?"

"All right then. Let's all vote for Esther and she will probably get it," Joe replied.

"I will vote for her if it's all done privately so no one will know who voted for whom," Irene said. "I don't especially like that girl, and this will probably give her more reason to act uppity if she wins it."

"She has my vote," Joe stated.

"And mine," Mandie added.

As they arrived at the schoolhouse, the four agreed to keep their decision secret.

When Mr. Tallant called the roll that morning, Mandie noticed that Tommy Lester was absent. He was probably grieving over the loss of his little brother or sister. No one had said whether it was a girl or a boy.

"We will now vote for the class poet," Mr. Tallant said, looking around the room. "I had thought about some class discussion on the poems written, but I don't believe we will have time for that. We'll just go ahead and vote. I'm sure you all remember what was read in class."

Mandie glanced at Joe, Faith, and Irene, and they all smiled.

The schoolmaster continued, holding up a stack of small papers. "I have pieces of paper for you to record your vote." He walked over to Leland, who sat at the desk nearest his, and handed the papers to him. "Leland, take one and pass the stack on down the line, each person taking one piece of paper."

As soon as everyone had one of the papers, Mr. Tallant explained, "Now I want you to write the name of the person you are voting for on your piece of paper, fold it once, and line up around the room and drop your papers in the basket on my desk."

"Yes, sir," came from around the room.

Mandie carefully wrote "Esther Rogan" on her paper, folded it, and got in line.

When all the votes had been cast, Mr. Tallant said, "Now I want you all to write down the names as I call them from these papers, and we'll see who received the most votes."

Mandie kept count and then turned to grin at her friends.

"The winner is Esther Rogan," Mr. Tallant announced. "Esther, will you please come forward?"

"Me?" Esther mumbled, rising from her desk. "I won?"

Then everyone began applauding and Esther became even more surprised.

"Up here, Esther," Mr. Tallant said as the applause finally died down. And when she finally got up to his desk, he said, handing her a large piece of paper, "Here is the certificate showing that you are class poet for the rest of the year. Your duties will consist of writing poems for the holidays and any special occasions we observe. Also, for the last day of school, during our closing ceremony, I'd like you to write a poem and stand and deliver it to the class and our visitors."

"Me, do all that?" Esther was still shaken up.

Mr. Tallant smiled. "It's easy. I'll help you."

As Esther returned to her desk, she mumbled, "But I didn't think my poem was that good."

Everyone laughed and then clapped. Esther finally joined in the laughter as she sat down.

Mandie let out a long breath and was silently thankful that she had not won.

After school was out for the day, Mandie and Joe walked with Faith to the crossroads.

"We will probably be back Thursday night, and I will see y'all at school on Friday," Faith told Mandie and Joe as she started to go on her way.

Mandie didn't speak but quickly hugged Faith and then turned to go on down the road toward her house.

As soon as they were out of sight of Faith, Joe said, "Mandie, Mrs. Chapman will probably get that job, so you might as well get used to the idea."

Mandie walked faster. "I know, I know, but I won't get used to it. I don't want Faith to move away."

Joe kept up with her and was silent until they came to the pathway leading to her house. He handed her books to her. "I'll see you in the morning." He turned to go back up the road toward his house.

"Yes," Mandie said, taking the books and hurrying down the pathway to her house.

She was trying hard not to cry. She didn't want Joe Woodard to see the tears in her eyes. "Oh, why can't Faith and her grandmother keep on living here at Charley Gap?" she mumbled, almost stumbling over Windy, who was coming to meet her. Mandie snatched up the kitten and held her so tight, she protested with a loud meow as Mandie carried her into the house.

For the next three days, Mandie didn't have much to say to anyone. She anxiously awaited her friend's return. Joe walked back and forth to school with Mandie, but he didn't talk either.

Finally Friday morning came, and Mandie was standing at the road, waiting for Joe. He came, walking fast, and she hurried forward to meet him.

"Did Mr. Miller bring them back last night?" Mandie asked anxiously.

"Yes, but I have not talked to Mr. Miller or to Faith and her grandmother. I don't know anything," Joe said.

"Then Faith will probably be at school today. Come on. Let's hurry," Mandie urged him as she walked faster.

They got to school early. Mandie waited and watched as everyone else arrived. Finally the bell rang and they had to take their seats. Faith had not shown up. Mandie listened as Mr. Tallant called the roll, and when he got to Faith's name, there was no answer.

"Faith Winters," Mr. Tallant repeated as he looked up from his desk.

Suddenly the door opened and Faith rushed inside, threw off her coat and hat, and hurried to her desk.

"Glad you got back, Faith," Mr. Tallant said, and continued with the roll.

Faith looked across the room and met Mandie's gaze. She smiled and Mandie felt her heart flip. If Faith was happy, that meant her grandmother had the job.

When the bell rang for recess, Mandie grabbed her lunch pail and rushed outside. Joe caught up with her and they sat on a log in the yard. She kept expecting Faith to join them.

Finally Joe spoke. "Faith is not eating with us. She is catching up on her assignments with Mr. Tallant and then will be going back home."

Mandie frowned. "How do you know?"

"I didn't rush out as fast as you did. I heard her talking to Mr. Tallant," Joe replied, biting into his ham biscuit.

"Did she say—" Mandie stopped and squeezed her biscuit in her hand.

"No, she did not say whether Mrs. Chapman got the job, at least not where I could hear. She asked Mr. Tallant to give her the assignments she missed because she was going back home," Joe said. "Seems her grandmother needs her for something or other this afternoon."

"Well," Mandie said, sighing.

Mandie and Joe were not sitting near the schoolhouse, and when Faith finally came outside she waved to them as she started down the trail to the road. "We got it!" she called with a big smile, but kept going.

Mandie almost choked on the bite of biscuit in her mouth. She swallowed it whole as she tried to blink back the tears in her eyes. She wouldn't look at Joe as she hastily put the rest of her food back in her pail.

Joe was silent.

When the bell rang to go back inside, Mandie stood up, shook out her long skirt, and took a deep breath as she picked up her lunch pail.

Joe, trying to lighten her mood, teased as they walked back toward the front door, "Do you still think I have a secret?"

Mandie frowned. "Are you going to tell me what it is?" she asked.

"Now, I didn't say I had a secret. I asked if you still *thought* I had one," Joe corrected, laughing.

"Why mention it if you're not going to tell me what it is?" Mandie asked as they stepped inside the schoolhouse.

"Now, that would be another secret in your opinion, wouldn't it?" Joe said, grinning as he went to his desk.

Mandie stomped her foot and went to sit down. Of course Joe Woodard had a secret. And she had not given up on trying to find out what it was. It was just that so many things were happening, she had not had time to really think about it.

Later, as the two walked home from school, Joe

said, "Today's Friday, so I suppose we won't be able to talk to Faith until Monday at school."

"Mrs. Chapman got the job. Didn't you hear her?" Mandie asked, not looking up at him.

"I heard her say that, but we still don't know all the details," Joe replied.

"Why do we need details? Faith is flat-out moving away from here. That's all that counts. She's going away," Mandie said loudly as she hurried on down the road.

Joe had to walk faster to keep up with her. "I'd like to know what the school looks like," he replied.

"A school is a school," Mandie said sullenly.

"But they're not all alike," Joe said. "I suppose I could talk to Mr. Miller tonight and find out about things over there at Tellico."

Mandie didn't answer. When they got to the pathway leading down to her house, she saw her father by the fence, talking to Mr. John Knight.

When Mr. Shaw looked up and saw the two, he came to meet them. "Mr. Knight here passed Mrs. Chapman's old house last night and he did see someone there—"

"He did?" Mandie interrupted.

"Yes, and I am telling you now not to go anywhere near that old house at any time, do you understand?" her father said.

Mandie took a deep breath. "Yes, sir, if you say so."

"I say so, loud and clear," Mr. Shaw said. "Until this matter is cleared up, I repeat, you are not to go anywhere near that house."

"Yes, sir," Mandie said.

Joe looked at Mr. Knight. "What did this person look like that you saw there, sir?"

Mr. Knight replied, "It was too dark to tell anything much, other than that he seemed to be tall and thin as Mrs. Clifton had said. I was just passing by on my way home and happened to look over into the yard. Evidently he also saw me, because he immediately disappeared behind the house."

"Did you follow him?" Mandie asked.

"No, I was in a hurry to get home," Mr. Knight replied. "But we know now that Mrs. Clifton wasn't imagining this. So some of us men plan on staking the place out this weekend."

"Can I go with you?" Joe asked.

"I don't think so, Joe. You'd have to get permission from your father before I'd allow it," Mr. Shaw said.

"Then I suppose I can't go either," Mandie said in a disappointed voice.

"That's right, Amanda," her father said. "We have no idea who this person is."

"Oh, shucks!" Mandie said.

"Just don't count on us catching him the first night we watch," Mr. Shaw said. "It may take several nights to find out who he is, because he may not be going over there every night."

Mandie thought about that until she went to bed that night. Then her mind returned to her friend, Faith. Her *former* friend, Faith, since Faith was moving away and leaving her.

Trying not to cry, Mandie wondered if her mother would allow her to go over and visit with Faith sometime this weekend so they could discuss everything about Tellico. Then she wouldn't have to wait until Monday to learn all the details.

But no, she was not going to do that. She was not anxious to find out when Faith was actually moving away. That could wait until Monday when they all went back to school. Besides, Faith and her grandmother were probably tired after their long journey and would want to rest for the weekend.

Mandie was going to miss her friend.

8

Just Wonderful!

MONDAY MORNING WHEN Joe came to meet Mandie, he was driving his mother's cart.

"Are we going to ride to school today?" Mandie asked as Joe stopped the vehicle at the pathway to her house.

Joe jumped down and took her books. "Come on, get in," he said. "I have to do an errand for my father."

As Mandie stepped into the cart, she said, "I hope it's not another mystery."

"No mystery," Joe said, getting back into his seat and picking up the reins.

Mandie waited, but Joe did not explain. "Well then, what is it?" she asked after a few seconds. The horse pulled the cart on down the road.

"Nothing, really," Joe replied. "Mr. Miller spent the night on watch over at Mrs. Chapman's old house. My father was supposed to pick him up this morning, but he had to go up the mountain to see a patient. So he asked me to go get Mr. Miller."

"How did Mr. Miller get over there? Doesn't he have a horse with him?" Mandie asked. Most of the men in the community got about on horseback.

"No," Joe replied. "He couldn't have a horse with him because he had to hide. If there's someone hanging around over there, they would see it and know somebody was there and they probably wouldn't stay."

"Well, whoever it is will certainly see us drive up in this cart," Mandie said.

"This person has only been seen at night. They will probably be gone by the time we get there," Joe answered.

"I hope not," Mandie said. "We might be able to find out who it is!"

"Amanda Elizabeth Shaw, remember what your father said. You are not to go investigating this thing yourself," Joe reminded her.

"I know, but since I'm going with you anyway, what difference would it make?" Mandie replied.

Joe frowned. "I probably shouldn't have brought you with me. Your father might think I am disobeying his orders."

"But your father asked you to go, and he knows you always walk to school with me," Mandie argued.

"Well, anyhow, here we are," Joe said, turning the wagon down the narrow trail that led to the old house. "Now, don't you go running off somewhere. You stay right here in the wagon while I look for Mr. Miller. My father said he was supposed to be hidden in the barn." He pulled the horse to a stop near the old barn and jumped down.

Mandie followed him. "I am not staying here in this wagon by myself," she said. "I'm going with you."

"All right then, but just make sure you stay right with me. Don't go wandering off somewhere," Joe firmly told her.

Joe hurried toward the entrance to the barn, and Mandie walked fast to keep up with him. She kept looking around the yard as she went, and at the big old house that Faith's grandmother, Mrs. Chapman, had inherited from a cousin. She saw signs of work having been done. The once-sagging back porch floor was now level. The huge rock chimney that ran up the side of the house had been falling apart, but now it seemed to be well stuck together and standing upright.

"Come on," Joe called back to her, stopping to wait.

"I'm coming," she said.

They entered the barn together, and Mandie immediately saw Mr. Miller asleep on a pile of hay in a far corner. "There's Mr. Miller," she said, pointing. "He's asleep."

"He was here all night, so I suppose he is sleepy," Joe said, going toward the man. "Mr. Miller, Mr. Miller."

Mandie had started to follow when out of the corner of her eye she saw someone swing down from the loft and run for the doorway. "Joe!" she called. "There he is! The man!"

Joe instantly ran after the man, with Mandie following. "Hey, mister, wait!" Joe called, following the man across the yard.

Mandie heard Mr. Miller behind them. "You go left and I'll go right, Joe," he called. She looked back and saw him running around the house in the direction the man had gone.

Joe ran the other way, and Mandie lifted her long skirts and followed. As they all came around to the front porch, Mandie saw the man pause and look at each of them. He looked young and rather handsome. He couldn't be a burglar. She ran right up to him as he stood there in surprise.

"Who are you?" she demanded.

Joe and Mr. Miller caught up with them.

"What are you doing on this property?" Mr. Miller asked.

The young man gasped for air. "I'm looking for my mother's cousin."

"And who might that be?" Mr. Miller asked suspiciously.

"Mr. Al Conley," the young man replied. He ran his fingers through his mussed dark curly hair.

"Mr. Al Conley? Why, he's been dead for years," Mr. Miller replied.

"Oh . . . I didn't know that," the young man said, his face falling.

"Exactly how did you know about Mr. Al Conley and not know he was dead?" Mr. Miller asked.

"My mother used to talk about him a lot. I'm sure she didn't know he had died. She had not seen or heard from him in years when she died back in December," he replied.

"Who was your mother? Where are you from?" Joe asked.

"My mother was Alicia McLendon. I'm Paul McLendon, and we lived in Kentucky, near Louisville. I don't have any other relatives," the man explained.

"Mr. Conley willed this place to Mrs. Chapman and her granddaughter, Faith. He was Mrs.

Chapman's cousin," Mandie told him. "Are they related to you also?"

Paul scratched his head, frowned, and said, "Not that I know of. Al Conley's mother was my mother's aunt."

"Then you and Mrs. Chapman aren't related, because she was kin to him on his father's side," Mandie said with a big grin as Paul smiled at her.

"According to rumor, you've been hanging around here awhile," Mr. Miller said. "What have you been doing for food?"

"I met up with some friendly Cherokee people a few miles back up in the mountains. I've been staying with them, coming over here now and then hoping to find Al Conley," Paul explained.

Joe suddenly looked at Mandie. "School! We're going to be late for school."

"Let's all get in the cart. I'll drop you all off at school, and I'll take this fellow here on to your father's house," Mr. Miller said.

"And whose house is that?" Paul asked.

"Joe is the son of the local doctor, Dr. Woodard, and I work for him," Mr. Miller explained. "Let's go."

"If this house was willed to those people you mentioned, why is it no one is ever here? I've watched and watched and never could find anyone home," Paul replied, following them to the cart.

"The men in the community have been doing work on this house and Mrs. Chapman and her granddaughter have been staying elsewhere until it's completed," Mr. Miller replied.

Mr. Miller drove down the road, and Mandie and Joe arrived at the front door of the schoolhouse just as the bell was being rung. Jumping down and running, they waved goodbye and stepped inside the door as the bell stopped ringing.

Mandie was disappointed to see that Faith was not there. She looked across the room at Joe and motioned toward Faith's empty desk. He frowned and nodded.

The day dragged as Mandie kept hoping Faith would come to school later. She never did.

When Mandie got home after school, she found her father working on the split-rail fence. She hurried to speak to him.

"Daddy," she called as she approached. "Have you heard about the man we found at Mrs. Chapman's house?"

Mr. Shaw stopped working and straightened up. "Yes, I heard. I told you, Amanda, I didn't want you poking around that old house," he reminded her.

Mandie bent her head. "I remember, Daddy, but I had to go because Joe was in the cart and had to go by and get Mr. Miller and we thought it would be safe with Mr. Miller there." She paused for breath. "Have you met the man we found over there?"

"No, I haven't," her father replied. "I only heard about him through Mr. Knight, who had stopped by the Woodards' this morning."

"Do you know if he is going to stay with the Woodards?" she asked.

"I don't know any more than you do," Mr. Shaw said, going back to his work on the fence. "Now, you get on inside and get your homework done."

"Yes, sir," Mandie replied, disappointed that he wouldn't talk. She started down the pathway toward the back door, turned, and called back, "I love you, Daddy." She waved and smiled.

Mr. Shaw once again straightened up from his work. He waved back with a big smile. "I love you, my little blue eyes."

Mandie went through the kitchen, where her mother was cooking, and on to the parlor to do her homework. Irene had not turned up yet. Maybe she would know something about the stranger.

Irene didn't get home until almost time for supper, and then all she could talk about was the fact that Tommy Lester would be back at school the next day because his mother was better. Irene had not even heard about Mandie and Joe finding the stranger at Mrs. Chapman's old house and was not interested.

The next morning Mandie hurried up to the road and was waiting for Joe when he finally came.

"You're late," she said as he approached.

"I know, so we'll have to walk fast," Joe replied, taking Mandie's books.

"Joe, tell me what happened to Paul McClendon," Mandie said, her short legs as always working hard to keep up with his long ones.

"Nothing," Joe said. "He's staying with the Millers until my father gets back, which should be sometime this afternoon. Mr. Miller thinks my father may give him a job and a place to live. My mother thinks so too."

"I'm glad, because he said he didn't have any relatives at all," Mandie said.

When they got to the crossroads, Mandie eagerly looked for Faith, but she was not there. Maybe she had gone ahead of them.

Just as Mandie and Joe stepped inside the schoolhouse and Joe handed Mandie her books, Irene and Tommy Lester came rushing in behind them, with Faith after them. But there was no time to talk then because they were almost late.

Mandie carried her books to her desk. As she sat down and started to put the books inside, she saw that the top book in the stack was a reading book, exactly like hers. She quickly examined the edges for the ink smudge she knew was on hers, but there was no smudge. She opened the cover, and there in bold ink was written "Property of Joe Woodard." She suddenly felt overcome with happiness. So this was Joe's secret. She looked across the room and held up the book.

Joe smiled and whispered loudly, "It took my mother all this time to find my old book."

Mandie saw Mr. Tallant look up from his desk, so she only mouthed her reply: "Thank you."

She was happy now. She finally had a reading book.

Faith stayed in at recess again, this time to take a test she had missed while she and her grandmother had been in Tellico.

"I'll walk with you and Joe after school," Faith promised as Mandie and Joe went outside to eat their lunch.

As soon as the bell rang for dismissal, Mandie and Joe hurried to get their coats. Faith joined them. Everyone crowded into the doorway, trying to get out first. Tommy and Irene were right behind Mandie when someone bumped into them, causing Tommy to drop his books. They slid beneath Mandie's feet. Mandie stooped to help Tommy retrieve them.

"I can get them," Tommy muttered as she began picking them up.

"I'll help," Mandie replied, picking up his reading book. Suddenly she saw an ink smudge on the top edge of the pages. She quickly flipped open the book, and there was her name. "This is my book!" she said in disbelief. Looking up at Tommy, who had stood up, she said, "You took my book, Tommy Lester!"

The crowd of pupils at the door suddenly became still. Mandie stood up, shaking with anger. "You took my book!" she repeated, holding the book open to her name.

Tommy quickly looked around the crowd and then at Mandie. "I'm sorry. I lost mine and never did find it. I was going to give it back to you, honest." His eyes filled with tears.

Joe spoke in Mandie's ear. "You don't need it now, Mandie, you have mine."

"Why did you take mine?" Mandie asked.

Tommy wouldn't look her in the eye. "I didn't have any money to buy another one because money had to be saved for the baby that was coming. I'm sorry we're so poor, and I'm sorry I took your book."

Mandie drew in a deep breath, thinking about the death of the little baby, and held her book out to Tommy. "Here, you can keep it. I have another one now, Joe's old one."

His head bowed, Tommy reached out and took the book. "Thank you," he mumbled as he slipped outside.

"Let's go, Mandie," Faith said behind her.

Mandie straightened her shoulders and smiled up at Joe. "Yes, let's go."

And on the way home, Mandie finally heard about Faith's visit to Tellico with her grandmother.

"My grandmother got the job," Faith told Mandie and Joe. "However, there are some strings attached to the offer. The position won't be available until fall, so my grandmother has not made a decision yet."

Mandie gave Faith a big smile. "I'm so glad she hasn't yet." Taking a deep breath, she added, "Just wait until you hear what Joe and I have to tell you."

Joe smiled at her as Faith said, "I've heard some

of it already. And he may not be directly related to us, but my grandmother is hoping he will consider us family, since he doesn't have anyone and we only have each other."

As they walked on, Mandie reached for Faith's hand and squeezed it. "Everything is turning out just wonderful."

Mandie's Bookplates

Nobody wants to lose a special book. Creating a special bookplate is one way to make sure that if your book does get lost, whoever finds it will know whom it belongs to.

Materials you will need:

drawer liner paper in a solid pale color
or light pattern

scissors

a ruler

a thin-tipped marker

glue (if your drawer liner paper does not have
adhesive backing)

books

1. Carefully measure, then cut your liner paper into several rectangles—3 x 5 inches is a nice size.
2. Personalize each rectangle. THIS BOOK BELONGS TO (your name) and FROM THE COLLECTION OF (your name) are good choices.
3. If your liner paper has adhesive backing, simply peel off the covering and place the paper on the

inside front cover of your book. Be sure to smooth it out carefully so that there are no air bubbles.

4. If your liner paper doesn't have adhesive backing, dab a tiny amount of glue—about the size of a nickel—on the back and spread evenly. Position as above.

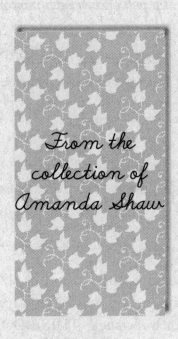

From the collection of Amanda Shaw

About the Author

LOIS GLADYS LEPPARD has written many novels for young people about Mandie Shaw. She often uses the stories of her mother's childhood in western North Carolina as an inspiration in her writing. Lois Gladys Leppard lives in South Carolina.

Visit the author's official Web site at www.mandie.com.